POKY and Friends™

The Haunted Tracks

By Bruce Talkington
Illustrated by DRi Artworks

A GOLDEN BOOK • NEW YORK
Golden Books Publishing Company, Inc., New York, New York 10106

 Library of Congress Catalog Card Number: 99-66764 ISBN: 0-307-16606-6 A MM First Edition 2000

The Mayor of Lower Trainswitch and Bill, the chief engineer, were unhappy. The trains were not running on time.

"Late again," sighed Bill as the 11:09 arrived at the station at 12:03.

"This *is* a problem!" agreed the Mayor as he studied his extra-large pocket watch.

Bill and the Mayor gathered the trains together. "You are running way too late," Bill told them.

"The ice cream is melting and the hot chocolate is getting cold," added the Mayor.

"But," protested one engine with a deep-throated whistle, "more and more of us trains have been working and there's only one set of tracks for all of us to use."

Bill held up a map. "I know," he said. "That's why we must use the tracks that run over the mountain."

"Regrettably," sighed the Mayor.

The older locomotives gasped with horror. "But those tracks are haunted," they moaned. "The last time a train went over those tracks all of its cargo disappeared!"

“I’ll ride on them first,” volunteered Tootle in his high-pitched tootling voice. “I’m not scared of any old train tracks.”

“It could be dangerous,” warned Bill, “especially for such a small train like you.”

“A train has to do what a train has to do,” said Tootle, puffing with determination, “no matter how big or small it may be.”

Bill didn't want to lose any more valuable cargo so he loaded empty cargo containers onto Tootle's boxcar. "Try to be back at 3:52," Bill said. "Then we'll make sure you still have your cargo on board."

"Remember," shouted the Mayor, "punctuality is the magic word."

Tootle knew he had to be brave and fast.
As he sped along the tracks, he chanted to himself,
"Don't be late. Don't be late.
Arriving on time makes a train great."

Soon Tootle found himself speeding around a sharp curve near the top of the mountain. He could feel the cargo in his boxcar slide as he leaned dangerously to one side. The little train gripped the tracks with his wheels, whispering these words:

"Keep your eyes on the track
And your wheels gripped tight.
This train won't be slowed
By any old fright."

The next thing Tootle knew, he was crossing a high trestle bridge. The bridge seemed to tremble under the little locomotive's weight, but still Tootle didn't stop. Instead he hummed to himself,

"A bridge may be high,
A bridge may be low,
Just stay on the track and go, go, go!"

As Tootle struggled over a steep hill, the cargo slid against the doors of the boxcar with a loud BANG! A frightened Tootle concentrated and said,

"Ever so high and ever so steep, a train on schedule must never creep."

The doors of Tootle's boxcar were starting to open! But before the cargo could fall out, Tootle began cannonballing down the other side of the hill.

"Clatters and clicks and clicks and clatters,
Being on time is all that matters."

As he charged through a long and dingy tunnel, Tootle's headlight caught sight of something. He pulled the brake to investigate. It was the missing cargo! Tootle quickly loaded it onto the boxcar. Before long he was on his way again.

Bill, the Mayor, and the other trains cheered as they saw Tootle heading into the station. Their cheers turned to gasps as they noticed the extra cargo on top of Tootle's boxcar.

"I found the missing cargo!" Tootle announced. "It must have fallen out of the last train that used those tracks. The tracks aren't haunted, they're just challenging. If we have sturdy locks on our boxcars and put signs on the tracks, everyone should be able to ride them."

SLOW—
DANGEROUS
CURVE
BRIDGE
AHEAD

So, that's exactly what they did.

A few weeks later, there was a ceremony for Tootle. "Thank you, Tootle," said the Mayor as he presented the train with a medal. "We are very grateful and proud. You are quite a locomotive for one so small."

Tootle smiled and tooted this tune:

"A train may be big, a train may be small,
but it's bravery that helps us all!"